ANIMAL

For Jasper, from your proud new mother
—J.B.

For my new best girl, Kristyn—
with love from Papa Dave
—D.McP.

Text copyright © 2005 by Jennifer Belle   Illustrations copyright © 2005 by David McPhail

ISBN 0-7878-1834-4   Printed in Singapore   Reinforced binding   Visit www.hyperionbooksforchildren.com

STACKERS

BY Jennifer Belle

PICTURES BY

David McPhail

HYPERION BOOKS FOR CHILDREN

NEW YORK

Aunt Alice and **M**ums warned me

Not

To make crumbs.

Bowls of porridge, but he

Eats my hot dog

Around the campfire,

Rrrrruns away!

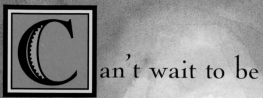

Can't wait to be
Alone in the house.
The sofa looks comfortable.

**D**own in Chinatown

Roaring at all who pass,

And accidentally passing

Gas as flames shoot

Out of her

Nostrils.

**E**xtremely

Large is an understatement.

Empties the

Peanut butter jar.

Have to

Ask very

Nicely

To keep him.

Fairy-tale prince.

Ribbit!

Only the lily pad

Gets annoyed.

**G**ets up,

Runs from his shadow

On February 2nd.

Under the shed

Nervously

Digging his

Hole.

Oh, it feels nice down here.

Great time for a nap!

Hop

On my saddle,

Ride,

Say *giddy-up*.

Exit the carousel gate.

I love your

Red hair.

I'll take you to the

St. Patrick's Day Parade.

Here, boy, sit. Okay,

Stand if you want to.

Every day we'll play,

Throw sticks,

Take walks.

Even when it

Rains.

Just

A big cat

Growling,

Until you

Agree to give him a ride in your

Rolls-Royce.

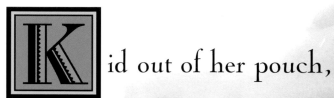**K**id out of her pouch,

A proud

New mother watches her baby.

Gracious, he's doing the

Australian crawl,

Right there with Koala

On the bank of the river.

Oh, is he clever!

Lonely, or

Are there any gentlemen bugs to

Date?

You look

Beautiful in your

Unusual dotted dress at the

Garden party.

My favorite

Old stoles have

Turned into

Holes.

Nobody so cute

Ever dashed up a

Wall

The way you do it.

**O**f course it is easy to see him.

Sandpipers stop

To stare.

Reason they can't understand it

Is how

Can

He breathe down there?

Please stop repeating the

Alphabet.

Reciting from A to Z.

Really, I already know it.

Oh, why can't you just say

Tweet tweet?

**Q**uiet as a clam,

Undisturbed,

Alone in her shell.

Has no pearls

Or posture.

Gladly sips salt water through a straw.

Ravenous, so he glares

And glowers.

Viciously

Eyes the nice children and

Nannies picnicking at London's Tower.

Shutting my eyes isn't helping, so

How can I fall asleep?

Even when I count

Each one of you ewes

Prancing over my sheets.

Think of the

Upside—you

Run faster than a snail.

Thank goodness you don't

Live in the

Empire State Building.

Upon a time,

Near the flowers

In the tapestry,

Comes to life,

Outrides the wind,

Returns the princess,

Never harmed.

Vladimir in the

Attic of the haunted house,

Misbehaving,

Playing

In the

Rafters with radar.

Enjoying mosquitoes,

Banging into walls,

Always wearing his

Tux.

Why do you hog every story

Of pigs and little girls?

Leave us alone! And by the way,

Furry fiend, you look silly in curls.

Xi'an is the name of the zoo

In China where the *xiongmao*,

Otherwise known as giant pandas,

Nibble the leaves of trees and

Get in a good game of

Mah-Jongg while keeping

An eye on their children, who

Only want to play Ping-Pong.

You always complain when she gabs

And gossips, and yet you have a

Knack for yakking right back.

Zoo is closing.

Everybody come see!

Baby is getting

Ready for bed.

A horse in striped pajamas.

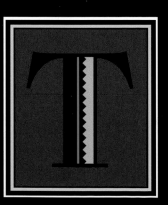
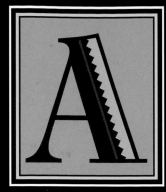
A
B

C

G

H

I

N

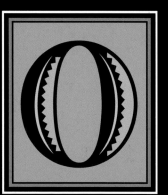
O
P

T

U

V

W